BEST SUPER BOWL RECORDS

by Paul Bowker

12 STORY LIBRARY

www.12StoryLibrary.com

12-Story Library is an imprint of Bookstaves.

Photographs ©: Bill Haber/Associated Press, cover, 1; Darron Cummings/Associated Press, 4; Joseph Sohm/Shutterstock.com, 5; Doug Mills/Associated Press, 6; Joseph Sohm/Shutterstock.com, 7; Bill Haber/Associated Press, 8; Super Bowl XXII/PD, 10; Al Messerschmidt/Associated Press, 11; Paul Sancya/Associated Press, 12; Images By Ian/Shutterstock.com, 13; Tony Tomsic/Associated Press, 14; Al Messerschmidt/Associated Press, 15; Mark Foley/Associated Press, 16; Erik Daniel Drost/CC2.0, 17; Gene Puskar/Associated Press, 18; dean bertoncelj/Shutterstock.com, 19; Harold Valentine/Associated Press, 20; Super Bowl XXIV/NFL/PD, 23; Elise Amendola/Associated Press, 24; Tony Tomsic/Associated Press, 26; dean bertoncelj/Shutterstock.com, 28; Au Kirk/CC2.0, 29

ISBN
978-1-63235-545-4 (hardcover)
978-1-63235-663-5 (ebook)

Library of Congress Control Number: 2018947730

Printed in the United States of America
Mankato, MN
June 2018

12 STORY LIBRARY

Access free, up-to-date content on this topic plus a full digital version of this book. Scan the QR code on page 31 or use your school's login at 12StoryLibrary.com.

Table of Contents

1

Super Bowl Records Are Shattered by Tom Brady

In 2017, New England Patriots quarterback Tom Brady worked overtime in Super Bowl LI. Brady led the Patriots to win in dramatic fashion. He smashed three Super Bowl passing records in one game.

Brady passed for 466 yards in the 34-28 victory over the Atlanta Falcons. His passing yardage broke the old record by 52 yards. Only Kurt Warner of the St. Louis Rams had passed for more than 400 yards in a Super Bowl game. Brady put the ball up 62 times. He completed 43 of the passes. Both were Super Bowl firsts.

Brady won the Super Bowl MVP award for the fourth time. He was the first to set that record. And he became the first quarterback to win five Super Bowls. The Patriots were the first to win a Super Bowl game in overtime.

THE FIRST OVERTIME

There had not been an overtime in fifty Super Bowl games. The New England Patriots and Atlanta Falcons ended that in 2017. Patriots running back James White scored a touchdown with 57 seconds left. The Patriots tied the score at 28-28 on a two-point conversion pass from Tom Brady to Danny Amendola. The Patriots won the game in overtime. White scored the game-winner on a two-yard touchdown run.

24

Number of records set in Super Bowl LI by the New England Patriots and Atlanta Falcons.

- Patriots quarterback Tom Brady passed for a Super Bowl record of 466 yards.
- Brady was the first to win four Super Bowl MVP awards.
- Brady became the first quarterback to win five Super Bowl games.
- The Patriots won the first overtime game in Super Bowl history.

2

Adam Vinatieri Makes Super Bowl History with Seven Field Goals

Adam Vinatieri of the Patriots began his Super Bowl run in Super Bowl XXXVI. The New England Patriots met the St. Louis Rams in 2002. The Rams were a 14-point favorite. The Patriots were trying to win their first Super Bowl.

The game was tied 17-17 in the final minute. Patriots quarterback Tom Brady led his team down the field. Vinatieri lined up for a 48-yard field goal with seven seconds left. He drilled the ball through the uprights. The Patriots won their first Super Bowl. Vinatieri was the hero.

It would not be the last time he won a Super Bowl game with a field goal. Vinatieri did it again two years later. He kicked a 41-yard field goal with four seconds left in Super Bowl XXXVIII. The Patriots defeated the Carolina Panthers by a score of 32 to 29.

That was just the beginning. Vinatieri became the first in Super Bowl history to kick seven field goals. He did so over five Super Bowl games with the New England Patriots and Indianapolis Colts. He is one of many to kick three field goals in one Super Bowl game. Don Chandler was the first to kick four field goals in one Super Bowl game. He did it for the Green Bay Packers in Super Bowl II.

3

Field Goals Vinatieri kicked for the winning points in his first three Super Bowls.

- Vinatieri kicked a 48-yard field goal on the game's final play.
- He became the first kicker in Super Bowl history to kick seven field goals in Super Bowl games in his career.
- Vinatieri played in Super Bowl games with both the New England Patriots and Indianapolis Colts.

3

Jerry Rice Sets Multiple Records in Four Super Bowls

8

Touchdown passes received by Jerry Rice in four Super Bowl games.

- Rice became the first receiver to catch three touchdown passes in one Super Bowl game. He did it twice.
- He was named MVP of Super Bowl XXIII after making 11 catches for 215 yards.
- Rice won three Super Bowls in seven years with the San Francisco 49ers.

Jerry Rice and the San Francisco 49ers didn't waste any time in Super Bowl XXIV. Rice went downfield for a pass. He crossed over the middle of the field. He caught the pass from Niners quarterback Joe Montana. Rice then fought off a would-be tackler and ran into the end zone. His touchdown was on the first San Francisco possession of the game.

It was the beginning of a historic day for Rice and the 49ers. Rice became the first receiver in Super Bowl history to have three touchdown catches in one game. The 49ers destroyed the Denver Broncos by a score of 55 to 10. Rice had seven catches for 148 yards in the 1990 game.

Rice helped the 49ers win three Super Bowl championships. He was named MVP in Super Bowl XXIII. He caught 11 passes for a record 215 yards in that game.

Rice played in four Super Bowls. His 33 catches in those games were a Super Bowl record. And so were his 589 receiving yards over those games.

ANOTHER IMPRESSIVE RECEIVER

James White of the New England Patriots was certainly a busy receiver in Super Bowl LI. He caught fourteen passes for 100 yards. The number of catches broke the Super Bowl record by one. White also rushed six times as a running back. He scored the game-tying touchdown with 57 seconds remaining. He scored the first overtime touchdown in Super Bowl history on a rush of two yards.

4

Rookie Timmy Smith Makes Record Super Bowl Debut

Timmy Smith received good news just prior to kickoff of Super Bowl XXII. It turned into a historic day for him and the Washington Redskins. It was also a big day for quarterback Doug Williams. He was told by Redskins coach Joe Gibbs before the game to tell Smith that he was starting in the 1988 game. Smith was a rookie running back. It was his first start in any NFL game. He responded in a big way.

Smith rushed for a Super Bowl record. He ran for 204 yards on 22 carries. He scored two touchdowns. His touchdown run of 58 yards was one of five touchdowns scored by the Redskins. The Redskins won by a score of 42-10.

Smith was not selected as game MVP because the day belonged to quarterback Williams. He became the first African-American quarterback to win a Super Bowl. Williams passed for 340 yards and four touchdowns.

ANOTHER ROOKIE DEBUT

Franco Harris of the Pittsburgh Steelers rushed for 158 yards and one touchdown. It was his Super Bowl debut in 1974. And just the start of a record career. He was the first running back to have more than 300 rushing yards in the Super Bowl. He ran for 354 yards in four Super Bowl games.

126

Yards rushed by Timmy Smith in seven games during the 1987 regular season.

- Smith rushed for 204 yards in his first start in the Super Bowl. Nearly double the yardage for the entire regular season.
- Smith learned of his start in the Super Bowl just prior to the game.
- He scored two touchdowns in his Super Bowl debut.

5

Willie Parker Runs Record-Breaking Super Bowl Touchdown

The play was called 34 Counter Pike. Willie Parker of the Pittsburgh Steelers ran the play to perfection in Super Bowl XL. He ran 75 yards for a touchdown. The touchdown helped the Steelers defeat the Seattle Seahawks by a score of 21-10 in the 2006 game. The run broke a Super Bowl record by just one yard. Marcus Allen of the Oakland Raiders had run 74 yards for a touchdown in Super Bowl XVIII.

The play came on the second play of the second half. The Steelers had a second down at their own 25-yard line. Tremendous blocking by the Steelers helped break Parker free for his record run. Center Jeff Hartings blocked the Seattle nose tackle. Tight end Heath Miller blocked a defensive end. Max Starks took out a linebacker. Parker found a hole and just kept running. The only thing he worried about was tripping and falling.

Parker played in two Super Bowl games. The second was Super Bowl XLIII with the Steelers. His longest run in that game was 15 yards. The Steelers won both games.

146

Yards run by Willie Parker in two Super Bowl games.

- Parker broke a record touchdown run for 75 yards.
- The run by Parker came on the second play of the second half.
- The touchdown run was the longest play of the game.

6

Rod Martin Sets Record for Interceptions in One Super Bowl

Rod Martin wanted to have an impact in his first Super Bowl game in 1981. Did he ever. Martin was a linebacker for the Oakland Raiders in Super Bowl XV. He intercepted Eagles quarterback Ron Jaworski three times. He made his first interception on just the third offensive play by the Philadelphia Eagles. It came on the first pass attempt by Jaworski. Martin set up a Raiders touchdown. The Raiders got the ball at the Eagles 30-yard line and quickly scored. The second interception came in the third quarter. The third interception happened with three minutes left in the game. It sealed a Super Bowl

victory for the Raiders by a score of 27-10.

It was an incredible game for a linebacker. Martin became the first player to have three interceptions in one game. And one of the few to have three Super Bowl interceptions in an entire career.

Martin still wasn't named Super Bowl MVP. That went to Raiders quarterback Jim Plunkett. He passed for 261 yards and three touchdowns. Martin played in a second Super Bowl game with the Raiders, XVIII. Another win for the Raiders.

Rod Martin talks to the media after his three Super Bowl interceptions.

THINK ABOUT IT

Rod Martin was not the Super Bowl MVP in Super Bowl XV. Do you think he should have been? What are your reasons for choosing Martin or quarterback Jim Plunkett?

14

Number of interceptions by Rod Martin over 12 seasons.

- Martin set a Super Bowl record with three interceptions in Super Bowl XV.
- All of the interceptions came against Philadelphia Eagles quarterback Ron Jaworski.
- Martin helped the Oakland Raiders to a 27-10 victory.
- Martin played in two Super Bowls with the Raiders.

7

L.C. Greenwood Still Holds Record for Sacks in One Super Bowl

In 1976, Dallas Cowboys quarterback Roger Staubach could not avoid L.C. Greenwood in Super Bowl X. Greenwood was a defensive end for the Pittsburgh Steelers in their heyday. He was a part of the defensive front four. They became known as the Steel Curtain. Also in the Steel Curtain were Joe Greene, Ernie Holmes and Dwight White.

Greenwood sacked Staubach four times in Super Bowl X. The Steelers

L.C. Greenwood sacks Dallas quarterback Roger Staubach in the first quarter of Super Bowl X.

MINISTER OF DEFENSE

Reggie White was known as the Minster of Defense. He was a dominant defensive lineman. He got three sacks in Super Bowl XXXI for the Green Bay Packers. White helped Green Bay defeat the New England Patriots. He was the second Green Bay Packer to get three sacks in one game. Willie Davis had three in Super Bowl II.

had seven sacks total. The Steelers defeated the Cowboys by a score of 21-17. It was the second consecutive Super Bowl victory for the Steelers.

Greenwood became the first to get four sacks in one Super Bowl game. More than 40 years later the record still stands.

Staubach was sacked again by Greenwood in Super Bowl XIII. The Steelers also won that game.

Greenwood won four Super Bowl games with the Steelers. They defeated the Cowboys twice.

5

Number of sacks by L.C. Greenwood over four Super Bowl wins with the Pittsburgh Steelers.

- Greenwood was a defensive end. He was part of the famous Pittsburgh Steel Curtain defense.
- Greenwood sacked Dallas Cowboys quarterback Roger Staubach a record four times in Super Bowl X.
- He helped the Steelers defeat the Cowboys in Super Bowl X, 21-17.

8

Jacoby Jones' Kickoff Return Covers Entire Field for a Super Bowl Record

164

Combined yards for two touchdowns by Jacoby Jones in Super Bowl XLVII.

- Jones returned the second half kickoff 108 yards for a touchdown.
- The touchdown helped the Ravens defeat the San Francisco 49ers.
- Jones also scored a touchdown on a passing play of 56 yards.

In 2013, Jacoby Jones provided a big spark for the Baltimore Ravens in Super Bowl XLVII. The Ravens were already ahead of the San Francisco 49ers at halftime. The score was 21-6. Jones returned the second half kickoff 108 yards. He scored a Baltimore touchdown. It was a Super Bowl record. The touchdown put the Ravens up by a score of 28-6.

Jones stood near the back of the Ravens end zone for the kick. It opened the second half. The ball was kicked deep into the end zone. He ran the ball out of the end zone. He went straight up the middle of the field. A number of blocks opened up the play. Jones sprinted ahead to score the touchdown. He was the first ever to return a kick more than 100 yards in a Super Bowl game. Jones also caught a touchdown pass covering 56 yards from game MVP Joe Flacco.

The Baltimore Ravens defeated the Niners by a score of 34 -31.

Jones's long play was originally ruled as a kickoff return covering 109 yards. That would have been an all-time NFL record. But the NFL later changed it to 108 yards.

The Ravens became the first team to have two kickoff returns for touchdowns in Super Bowls. Jermaine Lewis returned a kickoff 84 yards for a touchdown in Super Bowl XXXV.

9

Don Chandler Sets Record for Field Goals in One Super Bowl

Don Chandler was a championship kicker four times over. He won two Super Bowl titles with the Green Bay Packers. He also won two National Football League championships. One with the New York Giants and one with the Green Bay Packers. Those championships came before the Super Bowl existed.

Chandler made quick history in the Super Bowl. He kicked four field goals in Super Bowl II. It was a Super Bowl record in

WIDE RIGHT

There are many kicks that have won a Super Bowl. Scott Norwood of the Buffalo Bills goes down in Super Bowl history for missing one. In 1991, he missed a kick of 47 yards on the final play of Super Bowl XXV. It became known as the wide right kick. It would have made Buffalo a winner of the Super Bowl for the first time. Instead, the New York Giants celebrated their victory by one point.

133

Combined yards of four field goals kicked by Don Chandler in Super Bowl II.

- Don Chandler set a Super Bowl record with four field goals in Super Bowl II.
- Chandler helped the Green Bay Packers defeat the Oakland Raiders.
- Chandler also won Super Bowl I with the Packers.
- Ray Wersching matched the record in Super Bowl XVI.

January of 1968. It remains a record today, 50 years later. Chandler helped the Packers defeat the Oakland Raiders by a score of 33 to 14.

In 1982, Ray Wersching of the San Francisco 49ers equaled the achievement in Super Bowl XVI. He also kicked four field goals. Two in the final quarter. His longest kick was 40 yards. The 49ers defeated the Cincinnati Bengals by a score of 26-21.

10

Joe Montana Sets Multiple Records in Super Bowl History

Quarterback Joe Montana turned the Big Easy into the Easy Championship. The game was played in New Orleans. The city is known as the Big Easy.

The San Francisco 49ers destroyed the Denver Broncos in Super Bowl XXIV. They won the game by a score of 55 to 10. The points scored by the 49ers were the most in Super Bowl history.

The 49ers are one of just two teams to top 50 points in the first 51 Super

Quarterback Joe Montana and wide receiver Jerry Rice after winning Super Bowl XXIV.

Bowls. The Dallas Cowboys scored 52 points in Super Bowl XXVII.

Montana set a number of Super Bowl records in the game. He became the first quarterback in Super Bowl history to throw for five touchdowns. He passed for 297 yards. He was not intercepted. He was not sacked. His 13 consecutive pass completions set a record. Montana also set records for career pass completions and career passing yardage in four Super Bowls. Montana was named Super Bowl MVP for the second time in his career.

THINK ABOUT IT

Do you think that the combination of Joe Montana and Jerry Rice are the best quarterback and receiver team in Super Bowl history? Why or why not? Which quarterback and receiver would you choose?

8

Number of touchdowns by 49ers in Super Bowl XXIV.

- Joe Montana passed for a Super Bowl record of five touchdowns.
- The 49ers set a record for points scored in a Super Bowl game.
- The 49ers won their fourth Super Bowl. It was their second Super Bowl win in a row.
- Montana was named Super Bowl MVP for the second time in his career.

11

Records Fell Fast in Super Bowl XXII

Redskins quarterback Doug Williarms passed for a record 340 yards and was named Super Bowl MVP.

Super Bowl XXII required a calculator. That is how fast the records fell. The Washington Redskins met the Denver Broncos in the 1998 showdown.

The two teams combined for 929 yards of total offense. It was the only time in 51 Super Bowls that two teams reached 900 yards. The Redskins were the ones smiling at the end of the day. They defeated the Broncos by a score of 42 to 10. They piled up 602 yards on offense. And were the first to top 600 yards in a Super Bowl game. Only one other team had more than 500 yards in 51 Super Bowls. The San Francisco 49ers had 537 yards in Super Bowl XIX.

The Redskins scored 35 points in the second quarter. Another Super Bowl record was made.

Redskins quarterback Doug Williams passed for a Super Bowl record of 340 yards. Rookie running back Timmy Smith rushed for a record 204 yards. Wide receiver Ricky Sanders had a record of 193 receiving yards.

Broncos quarterback John Elway also joined in. He became the first quarterback in Super Bowl history to catch a pass. Elway caught a pass of 23 yards from running back Steve Sewell.

620

Combined passing yards by the Redskins and Broncos in Super Bowl XXII.

- The Redskins and Broncos combined for 929 yards of offense.
- The Redskins set a Super Bowl record with 602 yards of total offense.
- The Redskins defeated the Broncos by a score of 42 to 10.
- Broncos quarterback John Elway was the first in Super Bowl history to catch a pass.

12

The Dallas Cowboys Set Record for Super Bowl Penalties, Twice

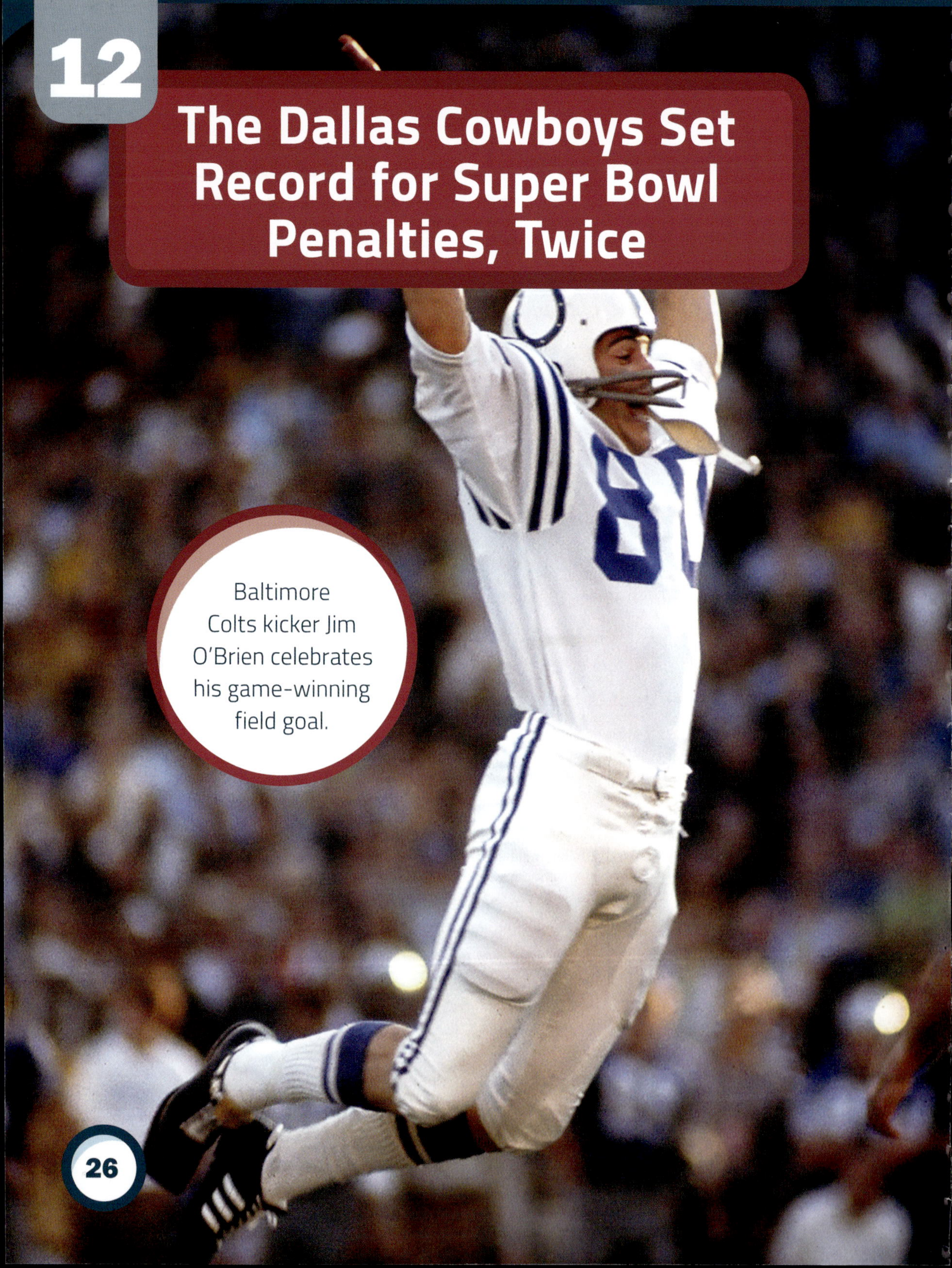

Baltimore Colts kicker Jim O'Brien celebrates his game-winning field goal.

Super Bowl V produced excitement. It was the closest game among the first 24 Super Bowls. Jim O'Brien kicked a 32-yard field goal with five seconds left. The Baltimore Colts won against the Dallas Cowboys, 16-13.

The game was also sloppy. The Cowboys set a Super Bowl record with 133 yards of penalties. That is not a record the Cowboys wanted to be known for. The record still stood more than 40 years after the 1971 game. The Cowboys lost. The penalties were just part of the problem. They had four turnovers.

The Cowboys set another Super Bowl record for penalties in Super Bowl XII. They had 12 penalties against the Denver Broncos. But the Cowboys managed to win that game by a score of 27-10. The Cowboys and Broncos were the first to combine for 20 penalties in one Super Bowl game.

THINK ABOUT IT

What do you think about all the penalties the Dallas Cowboys had? If you were the coach, would you bench a player who kept making penalties?

164

Combined yards of penalties by the Colts and Cowboys in Super Bowl V.

- Both teams combined for a Super Bowl record of eleven turnovers.
- The Cowboys set a Super Bowl V record with 133 penalty yards.
- The Cowboys set a record of 12 penalties in Super Bowl XII.
- The Cowboys and Denver Broncos were the first to combine for 20 penalties in a Super Bowl. They did it in Super Bowl XII.

Fun Facts and Stories

Using His Arm

Adam Vinatieri provided the winning kick for the New England Patriots in Super Bowl XXXVI. It was against the St. Louis Rams. He struck again in 2004. The teams met in a rematch during the regular season. Vinatieri began the game by kicking four field goals. Then he threw a touchdown pass on a fake field goal attempt. The Patriots won by a score of 40-22. In 10 years with the Patriots, that was the only pass Vinatieri ever threw.

Game Balls for Family

What happens to those cherished game balls after a Super Bowl game is over? Rod Martin has three of them from Super Bowl XV. He intercepted three passes for a Super Bowl record. The Oakland Raiders defeated the Philadelphia Eagles by a score of 27-10. He kept all three balls and put them in storage. He intends to keep them in his family. He is passing them on to his two daughters and grandchildren.

The Big Easy

Jacoby Jones is a native of New Orleans. So, when Jones and the Baltimore Ravens were preparing to play in Super Bowl XLVII in New Orleans, mom took over. Home cooking was just what the Ravens needed. Jones invited his teammates for a meal. His mom cooked up fish, potatoes, sweet corn and sausage. Also on the menu were stuffed bell peppers.

A Helping Hand

The San Francisco 49ers dominated the Denver Broncos in Super Bowl XXIV. They scored a Super Bowl record 55 points. Denver quarterback John Elway was sacked four times and intercepted twice. San Francisco linebacker Matt Millen helped Elway up after sacking him late in the game. Millen told Elway to keep his head up. "He told me, 'Hang in there.'" Elway said.

One Final Kick

Jim O'Brien of the Baltimore Colts missed a field goal and an extra point in Super Bowl V. The game featured the most penalties and turnovers in Super Bowl history. The Colts and Dallas Cowboys combined for 164 penalty yards. They also combined for eleven turnovers. O'Brien made up for his missed kicks. He kicked a 32-yard field goal with five seconds left. It won the game for the Colts by a score of 16 to 13.

Glossary

Big Easy
Another name for the city of New Orleans in Louisiana.

blocking
When one player gets in the way of another. Sometimes physically moving the player away. They may not hold or tackle the player.

debut
The first time a player performs in a game.

end zone
The portion of the field where touchdowns are scored. It is 10 yards long and located at both ends of the field.

interception
When a pass is caught by a player from the opposing team.

linebacker
A defensive player who is positioned behind the scrimmage line. They make tackles on both running and short passing plays.

MVP
Abbreviation for most valuable player.

overtime
The extra period played if the score is tied at the end of regulation play time.

quarterback
A player who runs the offense. They take the ball on a snap from the center. The quarterback usually passes the ball or hands it off to a running back.

rookie
A first-year player in the National Football League.

sack
When a defensive player tackles the quarterback in the backfield.

touchdown
When a player with the ball gets into the end zone. A touchdown scores six points.

For More Information

Books

Howell, Brian, *12 Reasons to Love Football*, Mankato, MN: 12-Story Library, 2018.

Adamson, Thomas K., *The New England Patriots Story*, Minnetonka, MN: Bellwether, 2017.

Wilner, Barry, *The Super Bowl*, SportsZone, Minneapolis, MN: Abdo Publishing, 2013.

Gitlin, Marty, *New York Giants*, SportsZone, Minneapolis, MN: Abdo Publishing, 2011.

Index

About the Author

Paul Bowker is an editor and author who lives on Cape Cod in South Yarmouth, Massachusetts. His 35-year newspaper career has included hundreds of NFL games. He is a national past president of Associated Press Sports Editors and has won multiple national writing awards.